For my husband, who never says Mine! Mine! Mine!
except when I try to take his car keys. —S.B.

To my cousin Akiko. —H.T.

Library of Congress Cataloging-in-Publication Data

Becker, Shelly.
Mine! mine! mine! / Shelly Becker; illustrated by Hideko Takahashi.
p. cm.
Summary: Grumpy Gail refuses to allow her visiting cousin Claire to play with her toys
or sit in her favorite chair, until her mother teaches Gail about sharing.
ISBN-13: 978-1-4027-2538-8
ISBN-10: 1-4027-2538-8
[1. Sharing—Fiction. 2. Cousins—Fiction. 3. Mothers and daughters—Fiction. 4. Stories in rhyme.]
I. Takahashi, Hideko, ill. II. Title.
PZ8.3.B39185Min 2006   [E]—dc22   2005034459

1 2 3 4 5 6 7 8 9 10

Published by Sterling Publishing Co., Inc.
387 Park Avenue South, New York, NY 10016
Text © 2006 by Shelly Becker
Illustrations © 2006 by Hideko Takahashi
Designed by Randall Heath
Distributed in Canada by Sterling Publishing
C/o Canadian Manda Group, 165 Dufferin Street,
Toronto, Ontario, Canada M6K 3H6
Distributed in the United Kingdom by GMC Distribution Services
Castle Place, 166 High Street, Lewes, East Sussex, England BN7 1XU
Distributed in Australia by Capricorn Link (Australia) Pty. Ltd.
P.O. Box 704, Windsor, NSW 2756, Australia

PRINTED IN CHINA
ALL RIGHTS RESERVED

Sterling ISBN-13: 978-1-4027-2538-8
ISBN-10: 1-4027-2538-8

For information about custom editions, special sales, premium and
corporate purchases, please contact Sterling Special Sales Department
at 800-805-5489 or specialsales@sterlingpub.com.

MINE! MINE! MINE!

BY **Shelly Becker**

ILLUSTRATED BY **Hideko Takahashi**

Sterling Publishing Co., Inc.
New York

My name is Gail and here's a tale
that I would like to share.
It happened when my cousin came—
my greedy Cousin Claire.

She kept on touching all my stuff
and getting in my way.
I told her, "All these toys are mine.
Find something else to play."

But Mother heard my every word
and said I should be nice.

"Go find a toy that she'll enjoy."
Yeah, that was Mom's advice.

My eyes began to scan the shelves
for something I could share.

Then suddenly, I turned to see
she'd snatched my teddy bear!

Well, then I snapped (I hadn't napped).
A fury filled my head.

I scowled so bad with eyes red mad,
and this is what I said:

"MINE, MINE, MINE! You give it back!
And stop that squeaky whine.
Let's get this straight now, Cousin Claire.
See all this stuff? It's MINE!"

"Those pickup sticks, that china doll,
this table set for tea,

the puzzle pieces, building blocks,
they all belong to me!"

"And even if you find it first,
don't touch it, don't you dare!

And by the way, you'd better move—
'cause that's my favorite chair!"

"No! Take me home!" Claire sobbed and moaned.
She said it wasn't fair.
So Mother had a "chat" with me
to teach me how to share.

"Gail, please be kind to Cousin Claire,"
Mom said. "It's easy, see?
Just watch how I share all day long
and try to copy me."

Her spools of thread,

her fresh-baked bread,

her slippers shaped like bunnies.

(My mother even shares her jokes
and some are kind of funny.)

I didn't care or want to share,
but Mother said I must.
I scrounged around until I found
some stuff, all full of dust.

An ugly hat, a broken bat,
a smelly, chewed-up shoe,
all battered, worn, and tattered, torn.
"Here, Claire. It's all for you."

"And here's a book, come take a look.
The front and back are green.

I liked it more before I tore
the pages in between."

"And how'd you like some bubble gum?
I'm sure it tastes divine.

There . . . stuck beneath that kitchen chair—
it's certainly not mine."

I felt so proud, I squealed out loud,
"I shared! I did it! Great!"
Claire glared at me, and I could see
she seemed a bit irate.

Well, I for one found sharing fun
and thought I'd try some more.
I offered Claire some spinach stew
and whoa—did she get sore!

She screamed and shrieked—completely freaked!
Her face was turning blue.
She gagged and coughed as if I'd offered
mothball-earthworm stew!

Mom said, "Come here, my darling dear.
There's one thing you should know—
you have to share your FAVORITE things,
and THEN you'll be a pro."

"The stuff I like? My shiny bike?
The games I love to play?
Well, how about I try that out . . .
tomorrow—not today?"

The time had come to drive Claire home.
We climbed into the car.
I said, "You'll see—someday I'll be
a sharing superstar."

"Yes, you'll get better
as you grow,"
my mom agreed with me.

"And sharing does
get easier.
Keep trying and you'll see."

Well, since that date, I'm sharing great!
And here's the proof of it:

You're looking at my favorite book
. . . and I don't mind one bit!